ANH DO

ILLUSTRATED BY
DAN McGUINESS

HOT DOG! 16

GARDEN TIME!

A Scholastic Press book
from Scholastic Australia

Scholastic Press
An imprint of Scholastic Australia Pty Limited (ABN 11 000 614 577)
PO Box 579 Gosford NSW 2250
www.scholastic.com.au

Part of the Scholastic Group
Sydney • Auckland • New York • Toronto • London • Mexico City
• New Delhi • Hong Kong • Buenos Aires • Puerto Rico

First published by Scholastic Australia in 2024.

Cover and internal design by Nicole Stofberg and Grace Felstead.

A catalogue record for this book is available from the National Library of Australia

ISBN: 978-1-76129-049-7

Typeset in YWFT Mullino.

Printed in China by RR Donnelley.
Scholastic Australia's policy, in association with RR Donnelley, is to use papers that are renewable and made efficiently from wood grown in responsibly managed forests, so as to minimise its environmental footprint.

10 9 8 7 6 5 4 3 2 24 25 26 27 28 / 2

ONE

Hello there!

This is my friend KEV.
QUICK, IT'S STARTING!

And that's **LIZZIE!**

We were watching one of our favourite TV shows about gardening. It was called **BERT'S BACKYARD.** Bert was a beetle who loved growing stuff!

'That looks like a **BEANSTALK!**' said Kev.

Lizzie looked sick. She hated heights.

'Whoa, look at that!' said Kev.

Bert was showing us his record-breaking **pumpkin**. It was as big as a barn!

'That would make one enormous **Halloween** pumpkin,' said Lizzie.

'Imagine how much pumpkin **soup** you could make,' said Kev. 'It'd be enough to feed our whole town **. . . for a week!**'

Next, Bert walked over to a row of tall yellow flowers.

'These ones follow the movement of the sun,' said Bert. 'Which is why they're called **SUNFLOWERS!**'

‘Maybe I’m a **SUN**-cat,’ said Kev. ‘I’m always following the sun too!’

My mum **LOVED SUNFLOWERS.**

Mother's Day was coming up and I'd just had a great idea for a gift. She would **LOVE** a bunch of sunflowers!

But I didn't have **MONEY** to buy her any . . .

'Ooh, yum!' said Kev, watching an ad for **HONEY** on TV. 'My mum **LOVES** honey. Maybe I could get her a big jar for Mother's Day!'

But then Kev looked glum. 'I can't afford to get her anything either . . .'

'**Strawberries!**' said Lizzie. Bert returned to the screen, showing viewers some of the juiciest and plumpest strawberries he'd grown. 'My mum **LOVES** strawberries!'

'I'd love to buy a big punnet for Mum for Mother's Day,' said Lizzie.

We **LOVED** our mums and really wanted to spoil them on their special day. But we'd have to come up with something else.

'Hang on a minute,' said Lizzie, pointing to the TV. 'Listen to this!'

At the end of the gardening episode, Bert announced a GREAT GARDEN CONTEST.

SEND YOUR PICS, AND THE GREATEST GARDEN ENTERED WILL WIN $100!

One hundred dollars?! That would mean sunflowers, honey and strawberries for all!

'Let's go to the garden!' I shouted.

TWO

We ran out to the front yard to have a look around. That prize money would be perfect!

But there wasn't much of a garden. Just a bunch of dry dirt, rocks and weeds . . .

'This will **NOT** win us that prize,' I said, sadly.

I'M *ROOTING* FOR YOU!

Our garden was way too plain and empty to enter in the competition.

'What's the **BUZZZZZZZ?**' said a bee and his family, as they were flying by our yard.

'We really want to build a great garden,' I said, looking at the weeds, 'but we don't have much to work with!'

The bee's name was Benny. He was with his family, flying up and down the street, searching for **FLOWERS** to turn into honey.

'Flowers are really hard to find these days,' he said.

Benny Bee and his family were part of a **HIVE** just down the road. They'd been having a tough time finding flowers . . . which meant no nectar for making **HONEY!**

Benny introduced us to his kids, Bob-bee, Ru-bee and Shell-bee.

'We would **LOVE** to buy more flowers and seeds to plant here,' said Kev. 'To make our garden nicer.'

'But it all costs money,' said Lizzie. 'Which we don't have!'

'Well,' said Benny, 'there IS a **COMMUNITY GARDEN** at the local park. They have some flowers, and they're always after volunteer helpers.'

Gardens do make the world a nicer place to live in!

THREE

It was a beautiful morning, perfect for a day at the park . . . and working in the garden!

‘Are you three here to volunteer?’ asked a friendly-looking squirrel.

We nodded, eagerly.

'Pop on some gloves and join me,' said Mrs Squirrel, as she led us over to a big pile of fresh soil. 'We're going to work on this **FLOWER BED** today.'

'Flower bed?' said Kev. 'We're having a **SLEEPOVER?** I'll grab the popcorn!'

Mrs Squirrel laughed. 'No, we call this a **BED**, but it's not for sleeping! It's where you three are going to plant some flower seeds!'

Ooh, this was so exciting!

'So what are we planting?' I asked.

'It's a surprise,' said Mrs Squirrel. 'I'll show you how to plant the seeds and care for them . . . and when they **GROW**, you'll find out what they are!'

'Kind of like winding up a Jack-in-the-box,' said Kev.

'What if the seeds grow into a **VENUS FLY TRAP?**' said Lizzie. 'And it tries to take a **BITE** out of us?'

'That could be pretty cool,' said Kev, dreamily . . .

'Or what if we grew a cactus?!' I suggested.

Mrs Squirrel gave us a bunch of seeds and showed us how to **PLANT** them.

First we **DUG** a row of little holes in the soil . . .

. . . then popped in the **SEEDS!**

Gave it all a sprinkle of **WATER** . . .

. . . and then we waited.

And waited.

And waited.

'Hey, I said this **ISN'T** a bed for sleeping!' said Mrs Squirrel.

The community garden was so cool. There were helpers potting, planting, trimming, watering . . . and even **SINGING!**

We wandered down the path to a big veggie patch.

THESE ARE OUR TOMATO VINES . . . AND CUCUMBERS . . . ZUCCHINI . . .
YOU GROW, GIRL!
OUR ROWS OF CARROTS . . . LETTUCE . . . AND BEETROOT!

Next, we were given the job of looking after some **BERRY PLANTS.**

'Maybe I need to clean my glasses, but I don't see any berries,' said Kev.

'First of all,' said Mrs Squirrel, 'the white flowers **TURN INTO** berries. And second of all . . .'

'Oh right, I forgot,' said Kev with a shrug.

'These plants are growing really quickly and **NEED MORE SPACE,**' said Mrs Squirrel. 'It gets tight in these little pots. Imagine growing too big for your house!'

Mrs Squirrel gave us each a pot, and asked us to plant them in the ground.

We worked away with our little shovels and plants . . .

. . . and soon we were ready to show Mrs Squirrel what we'd done!

She put her hands on her hips, checked out the plants . . . and chuckled.

Interesting? What did that mean?

Turns out, I'd accidentally planted mine **WAY TOO CLOSE** to the side of the box.

Lizzie had planted the **WHOLE POT!**

And Kev had planted his **UPSIDE DOWN!**

We picked up our shovels and tried again!

This time, we hoped Mrs Squirrel would be much happier with our effort!

When we were given a proud nod of approval . . .

. . . we were happy-dancing too!

GARDENING WAS FUN!

WHEN THE GROWING GETS TOUGH, THE TOUGH GET GROWING!

FOUR

After spending a whole week working in the community garden, we felt like real **GREEN THUMBS!**

No, we haven't really turned green! That's just what you call people who love to garden!

The berries were growing **BIG** and **JUICY . . .**

. . . and the flowers were almost ready to
BLOOM.

All the veggies were growing well too.
Everything in the garden looked great.

Now it was time to help Mrs Squirrel pack up some plants to take to the **MARKET.**

We loaded baskets of corn, lettuce, beetroot, tomatoes . . . and plenty of flowers.

Mrs Squirrel **THANKED US** for all of our help.

'You've been amazing,' she said, 'and you've all become **EXCELLENT GARDENERS.'**

'Thanks, Mrs Squirrel,' we said.

'You know what?' she added. 'We have **TOO MUCH** to take to the market.'

Our own garden?! My friends looked as excited as me!

Yes, please!

We loaded our wagon and headed home with our big collection. We couldn't wait to get to work on making our garden special, with everything we'd learned from Mrs Squirrel.

In the yard, we used a hoe to start loosening up the soil, getting it ready for the plants.

We carefully planted the flowers in one bed . . . and the berries and veggies in another.

Finally, we stood back to admire it all.

'I think it needs one more thing,' said Kev.

We were busy laughing at Kev the **SCARECAT** when we heard a familiar buzzing sound.

BUZZZZZ ZZZZZZ...

Benny Bee and his family were back!

'Your garden looks wonderful!' Benny said. 'Doesn't it, kids?'

We felt proud. We had a great garden, the sun was shining and . . .

LOOK!

The flowers were opening!

Could I spot a hint of golden-yellow?

SUNFLOWERS! MY MUM'S FAVOURITE!

The bees were **THRILLED** that there were loads of flowers on our street now!

The garden looked **GREAT,** especially now that the sunflowers had opened! But was it great enough to enter the Bert's Backyard contest?

We had no idea, but took some pics to give it a go!

Our new friends, the bees, came over the next day for the announcement of the **WINNER** of the Bert's Backyard Great Garden Contest!

Before Bert showed everyone the winning pic, we leaned in and held our breath.

COME ON, COME ON, COME ON . . .

We **REALLY** wanted that prize money to buy gifts for Mother's Day!

But the winning garden was **NOT** ours . . .

That chook had *some* garden!

'Sorry you didn't win, gang,' said Benny Bee. 'But look how cool your garden is! We **LOVE** it, don't we, kids?'

The kids buzzed happily.

Betty Bee buzzed over to cheer us up. It didn't matter that we didn't win, she told us.

'There are **FLOWERS** growing for Hotdog to give to his mum,' she said. 'There are **STRAWBERRIES** in the veggie patch for Lizzie's mum.'

'And now we have a beehive full of **HONEY,**' added Benny. 'Kev, you can give some to **YOUR** mum.'

They were right, our yard was full of goodness! We couldn't wait to share our hard work with our mums!

FIVE

It was Mother's Day, at last! ALL of our mums were coming over later for a Garden Party.

We had baked a big **ZUCCHINI** slice, yummy **CARROT** cake, and a whole slab of **BEETROOT** brownies!

We ran outside to start setting up our yard.

But we couldn't believe what we found . . .

ALL of our flowers, berries and veggies were **GONE!**

Someone had taken everything!

I barely noticed the growing buzzing over the sound of my sniffles.

Benny and the bees had come over to give us the jar of **HONEY** for Kev's mum.

'What happened?!' said Benny as he looked around our empty yard.

'We have no idea,' I explained. 'Everything's missing . . . someone must have **STOLEN** it all.'

'Hang on,' said Shell-bee. 'I am pretty sure I saw a **ROOSTER** and a **DONKEY** riding past on their bikes earlier. They were carrying loads of flowers . . .'

ROOSTER AND DONKEY!

We couldn't believe it! Rooster and Donkey were up to their nasty tricks again!

'Do you have any idea **WHICH WAY** they were going?' I asked.

Shell-bee hummed for a moment. 'It looked like they were riding to the park,' she said.

'I bet they're on their way to the community garden to **PINCH MORE** flowers!' said Lizzie.

All of us set off faster than a
CHEETAH ON ROLLERBLADES!

Once we reached the park, we skidded to a stop and **SURPRISE, SURPRISE** . . . Rooster and Donkey were in the Community Garden **CUTTING** the flowers!

'HEY!' Lizzie shouted. **'STOP RIGHT THERE!'**

Donkey looked up and saw us. 'Time to leave!' he hissed to Rooster.

Rooster and Donkey fled as fast as they could. We were chasing them, but they were **WAY TOO QUICK FOR US.**

BUT NOT TOO QUICK FOR OUR BEE FRIENDS!

The bees darted through the air and chased down Rooster and Donkey.

'What is that?!' squealed Donkey, looking up at the bees in pursuit.

'BEES!' shrieked Rooster. He wasn't looking where he was going . . .

Donkey **TRIPPED OVER** Rooster and landed face-first in a bucket!

Rooster and Donkey scrambled to each other. They looked **RATTLED!** They were cowering and swatting the air!

The bees started circling faster and faster. Soon, they were almost like a **TORNADO** around the thieves!

Their buzzing was **VERY LOUD** too!

BZZZZZZZZ!

'It sure is **SWARM** out here today!' buzzed Benny.

'Please don't sting us!' Donkey cried.

'Let us go!' cried Rooster. 'You can have everything back! **EVERYTHING!**'

Slowly the bees stopped speeding around them. The buzzing grew quiet.

'We stole everything, okay,' said Donkey. 'We wanted to sell the flowers and veggies so we could afford . . .'

Surely they weren't after something for their mums for Mother's Day too?

'. . . afford **LOLLIES,**' said Rooster.

LOLLIES?!

Who doesn't love lollies? But stealing was not the way to get a sweet treat!

While the bees hovered high like a **BUZZING** black cloud, Rooster and Donkey gave **EVERYTHING** back . . .

Then they wandered away, gloomily. Empty-handed.

'Thanks for stopping those bad guys!' Mrs Squirrel said to the bees. She'd been busy in the greenhouse and had only just realised what had happened.

'Thank **YOU** for planting so many flowers here!' said Benny and Betty Bee. 'It makes life **MUCH SWEETER** for us and our hive!'

'Great work, everyone!' I said.

'Now we have a

GARDEN PARTY

to get ready for!'

SIX

Back home, we thanked the bees again.

Benny and his family thanked **US** for planting flowers so that they could keep making that sweet, sweet honey!

We said goodbye to our friends and started getting ready for our party . . .

We set up a big table and chairs with all of our **TREATS AND GIFTS!**

Just in time for our mums to arrive!

'MUM!' I ran to her as quickly as my little legs could manage.

'Hotdog!' said Mum, before lifting me into a huge hug.

Which reminded me . . .

'Mum, I have a present for you!' I said.

'SUNFLOWERS!' she said. 'My favourite!'

‘I have a present for you too, Mum,’ said Kev to his mum, who’d come all the way to visit from Rainbow Island.

'Oh, **HONEY BUNNY,**' said Kev's mum, before giving him a big kiss on the cheek.

'And I haven't forgotten **MY** mum,' said Lizzie.

'Oh, you're **BERRY, BERRY** sweet,' said Lizzie's mum, and the pair cuddled.

Our mums **LOVED** their gifts, and they were **SO PROUD** when they realised we'd grown the flowers and berries ourselves.

Plus we'd grown the veggies we'd used to make our lunch!

'It's not always about the gift,' said my mum.

'But I sure do **LOVE** my gift . . .' she added.

We were pretty proud of ourselves too.

FLOWER POWER!

MORE ADVENTURES COMING SOON!

COLLECT THEM WHILE
THEY'RE HOT!
ANH DO
HOT DOG!
ANH DO
HOT DOG! PARTY TIME! 2
ANH DO
HOT DOG! CIRCUS TIME! 3
ANH DO
HOT DOG! GAME TIME! 4
ANH DO
HOT DOG! CAMPING TIME! 5
ANH DO
HOT DOG! MOVIE TIME! 6
ANH DO
HOT DOG! SHOW TIME! 7
ANH DO
HOT DOG! ART TIME! 8
ANH DO
HOT DOG! SNOW TIME! 9
ANH DO
HOT DOG! BEACH TIME! 10
ANH DO
HOT DOG! TOOL TIME! 11
ANH DO
HOT DOG! LOLLY TIME! 12
ANH DO
HOT DOG! SOCCER TIME! 13
ANH DO
HOT DOG! TIDY TIME! 14
ANH DO
HOT DOG! TOY TIME! 15
ANH DO
HOT DOG! GARDEN TIME! 16
SCHOLASTIC